SCARED

For Thelma Fown –

to read in the moonlight.

Orchard Books
338 Euston Road, London NW1 3BH
Orchard Books Australia
Hachette Children's Books
Level 17/207 Kent Street, Sydney, NSW 2000

First published by Orchard Books in 1999 or 2000
This edition published in 2008
Text copyright © Anthony Horowitz 1999

A CIP catalogue record for this book is available from the British Library

ISBN 978 1 84616 968 7

5 7 9 10 8 6

www.orchardbooks.co.uk

Printed and bound in Great Britain by CPI Bookmarque, Croydon, CR0 4TD

Orchard Books is a division of Hachette Children's Books,
an Hachette Livre UK company.

About the Author

Anthony Horowitz was brought up on horror stories, and his childhood love of all things sinister and scary has stayed with him. The stories in this book are inspired by ordinary, everyday objects and events, as are most of the stories in the rest of the series. But each of them has a twist to remind us that even in a safe, predictable world, the horrible and unexpected, the blood-curdling and the spine-chilling, are never far away.

Anthony Horowitz is the highly successful author of a bestselling range of books, including detective stories, adventure stories and spy stories which have been translated into over a dozen languages. He is also a well-known television screenwriter with credits including *Poirot*, *Midsomer Murders* and *Foyle's War*. Anthony lives in East London.

'A first class children's novelist'
TIMES EDUCATIONAL SUPPLEMENT

'Perfect for readers with an appetite for ghoulish happenings'
SCHOOL LIBRARIAN ASSOCIATION

'Suspenseful and exciting'
BOOKS FOR KEEPS

46 272 896 6

ANTHONY HOROWITZ

SCARED

ORCHARD BOOKS

Contents

SCARED

Gary Wilson was lost.

He was also hot, tired and angry. As he slogged his way through a field that looked exactly the same as the last field and exactly the same as the one ahead, he cursed the countryside, his grandmother for living in it, and above all his mother for dragging him from their comfortable London house and dumping him in the middle of it. When he got home he would make her suffer, that was for sure. But where exactly was home? How had he managed to get so lost?

He stopped for the tenth time and tried to get his bearings. If there had been a hill he would have climbed it, trying to catch sight of the pink cottage where his grandmother lived. But this was Suffolk, the flattest county in England, where country lanes could lie perfectly concealed behind even the shortest length of grass and where the horizon was always much further away than it had any right to be.

Gary was fifteen years old, tall for his age, with the permanent scowl and narrow eyes of the fully qualified school bully. He wasn't heavily built – if anything he was on the thin side – but he had long arms, hard fists, and he knew how to use them. Maybe that was what made him so angry now. Gary liked to be in control. He knew how to look after himself. If anyone had seen him, stumbling around an empty field in the middle of nowhere, they'd have laughed at him. And of course he'd have had to pay them back.

Nobody laughed at Gary Wilson. Not at his name, not at his place in class (always last), not at the acne which had recently exploded across his face. Generally people avoided him, which suited Gary fine. He actually enjoyed hurting other kids, taking their lunch-money or ripping pages out of their books. But scaring them was just as much fun. He liked what he saw in their eyes. They were scared. And Gary liked that best of all.

About a quarter of the way across the field, Gary's foot found a pot-hole in the ground and he was sent sprawling with his hands outstretched. He managed to save himself from falling but a bolt of pain shot up his leg as his ankle twisted. He swore silently, the four-letter word that always made his mother twitch nervously in her chair. She had long since stopped trying to talk him out of using bad language. He was as tall as her now and he knew that in her own, quiet way, she was scared of him too. Sometimes she would try to reason with him, but for her the time of telling had long since passed.

He was her only child. Her husband – Edward Wilson – had been a clerk at the local bank until one day, quite suddenly, he had fallen over dead. It was a massive heart attack, they said. He was still holding his date-stamp in one hand when they found him. Gary had never got on with his father and hadn't really missed him – particularly when he realised that he was now the man of the house.

The house in question was a two-up, two-down, part of a terrace in Notting Hill Gate. There were insurance policies and the bank provided a small pension so Jane Wilson was able to keep it. Even so, she'd had to go back to work to support Gary and herself...no need to ask which of the two was the more expensive.

Holidays abroad were out of the question. As much as Gary whined and complained, Jane Wilson couldn't find the money. But her mother lived on a farm in Suffolk and twice a year, in the summer and at Christmas, the two of them made the two-hour train journey up from London to Pye Hall just outside the little village of Earl Soham.

It was a glorious place. A single track ran up from the road past a line of poplar trees and a Victorian farmhouse and on through a gap in the hedge. The track seemed to come to an end here but in fact it twisted and continued on to a tiny, lopsided cottage painted a soft Suffolk pink in a sea of daisy-strewn grass.

'Isn't it beautiful?' his mother had said as the taxi from the station had rattled up the lane. A couple of black crows swooped overhead and landed in a nearby field.

Gary had sniffed.

'Pye Hall!' His mother had sighed. 'I was so happy here once.'

But where was it?

Where was Pye Hall?

As he crossed what he now realised was a quite enormous field, Gary found himself wincing with every step. He was also beginning to feel the first stirrings of…something. He wasn't actually scared. He was too angry for that. But he was beginning to wonder just how much further he would have to walk before he knew where he was. And how much further *could* he walk? He swatted at a fly that was buzzing him and went on.

Gary had allowed his mother to talk him into coming, knowing that if he complained hard enough she would be forced to bribe him with a handful of CDs – at the very least. Sure enough he had passed the journey from Liverpool Street to Ipswich listening to *Heavy Metal Hits* and had been in a good enough mood to give his grandmother a quick peck on the cheek when they arrived.

'You've grown so much,' the old lady had

exclaimed as he slouched into a battered armchair beside the open fireplace in the front room. She always said that. She was so boring.

She glanced at her daughter. 'You're looking thinner, Jane. And you're tired. You've got no colour at all.'

'Mother, I'm fine.'

'No, you're not. You don't look well. But a week in the country will soon sort you out.'

A week in the country! As he limped onward and onward through the field, swatting again at the wretched fly that was still circling his head, Gary thought longingly of concrete roads, bus stops, traffic lights and hamburgers. At last he reached the hedge that divided this field from the next and he grabbed at it, tearing at the leaves with his bare hands. Too late, he saw the nettles behind the leaves. Gary yowled, bringing his clenched hand to his lips. A string of white bumps rose up, scattered across the palm and insides of his fingers.

What was so great about the country?

Oh, his grandmother went on about the peace,

the fresh air, all the usual rubbish spouted by people who wouldn't even recognise a zebra crossing if they saw one. People with no life at all. The flowers and the trees and the birds and the bees. Yuck!

'Everything is different in the country,' she would say. 'You float along with time. You don't feel time rushing past you. You can stand out here and imagine how things were before people spoiled everything with their noise and their machines. You can still feel the magic in the countryside. The power of Mother Nature. It's all around you. Alive. Waiting...'

Gary had listened to the old woman and sneered. She was obviously getting senile. There was no magic in the countryside, only days that seemed to drag on for ever and nights with nothing to do. Mother Nature? That was a good one. Even if the old girl *had* existed – which was unlikely – she had long ago been finished off by the cities, buried under miles of concrete motorway. Driving along the M25 at 100 m.p.h. with the roof open and the CD player on full volume...to Gary, *that* would be real magic.

After a few days lazing around the house, Gary

had allowed his grandmother to persuade him to go for a walk. The truth was that he was bored by the two women and, anyway, out in the fields he would be able to smoke a couple of the cigarettes he had bought with money stolen from his mother's handbag.

'Make sure you follow the footpaths, Gary,' his mother had said.

'And don't forget the country code,' his grandmother had added.

Gary remembered the country code all right. As he ambled away from Pye Hall he picked wild flowers and tore them to shreds. When he came to a gate he deliberately left it open, smiling to himself as he thought of the farm animals that might now wander on to the road. He drank a Coke and span the crumpled can into the middle of a meadow full of buttercups. He half snapped the branch off an apple tree and left it dangling there. He smoked a cigarette and threw the butt, still glowing, into the long grass.

And he had strayed off the footpath. Perhaps that

hadn't been such a good idea. He was lost before he knew it. He was tramping through a field, crushing the crop underfoot, when he realised that the ground was getting soft and mushy. His foot broke through the corn or whatever it was and water curled over his shoe, soaking into his sock. Gary grimaced, thought for a moment and decided to go back the way he had come...

Only the way he had come was somehow no longer there. It should have been. He had left enough landmarks after all. But suddenly the broken branch, the Coke tin and the torn-up plants had vanished. Nor was there any sign of the footpath. In fact there was nothing at all that Gary recognised. It was very odd.

That had been over two hours ago.

Since then, things had gone from bad to worse. Gary had made his way through a small wood (although he was sure there hadn't been a wood anywhere near Pye Hall) and had managed to scratch his shoulder and gash his leg on a briar. A moment later he had backed into a tree which had torn his favourite jacket, a black and white striped blazer that he had shop-lifted from an Oxfam shop in Notting Hill Gate.

He had managed to get out of the wood – but even that hadn't been easy. Suddenly he had found a stream blocking his path and the only way to cross it had been to balance on a log that was lying in the middle. He had almost done it too but at the last minute the log had rolled under his foot, hurling him backwards into the water. He had stood up spluttering and swearing. Ten minutes later he had stopped to have another cigarette but the whole packet was sodden, useless.

And now…

Now he screamed as the insect, which he had assumed was a fly but which in fact was a wasp, stung him on the side of the neck. He pulled at his damp and dirty Bart Simpson T-shirt, squinting down to see the damage. Out of the corner of his eye he could just make out the edge of a huge, red swelling. He shifted his weight on to his bad foot and groaned as fresh pain shuddered upwards. Where was Pye Hall? This was all his mother's fault. And his grandmother's. They were the ones who'd suggested the walk. Well, they'd pay for it. Perhaps they'd think twice about how lovely the countryside was when they saw their precious cottage go up in smoke.

And then he saw it. The pink walls and slanting chimneys were unmistakable. Somehow he had found his way back. He only had one more field to cross and he'd be there. With a stifled sob, Gary set off. There was a path of sorts going round the side of the field but he wasn't having any of that. He walked straight across the middle. It had only just been sown. Too bad!

This field was even bigger than the one he had just crossed and the sun seemed to be hotter than ever. The soil was soft and his feet sank into it. His ankle was on fire and, every step he took, his legs seemed to get heavier and heavier. The wasp wouldn't leave him alone either. It was buzzing round his head, round and round, the noise drilling into his skull. But Gary was too tired to swat at it again. His arms hung lifelessly in their sockets, his fingertips brushing against the legs of his jeans. The smell of the countryside filled his nostrils, rich and deep, making him feel sick. He had walked now for ten minutes, maybe longer. But Pye Hall was no closer. It was blurred, shimmering on the edge of his vision. He wondered if he was suffering from sunstroke. Surely it hadn't been as hot as this when he set out?

Every step was becoming more difficult. It was as if his feet were trying to root themselves in the ground. He looked back (whimpering as his collar rubbed the wasp sting) and saw with relief that he was exactly halfway across the field. Something ran down his cheek and dripped off his chin – but whether it was sweat or a tear he couldn't say.

He couldn't go any further. There was a pole stuck in the ground ahead of him and Gary seized hold of it gratefully. He would have to rest for a while. The ground was too soft and damp to sit on so he would rest standing up, holding on to the pole. Just a few minutes. Then he would cross the rest of the field.

And then...

And then...

When the sun began to set and there was still no sign

of Gary, his grandmother called the police. The officer in charge took a description of the lost boy and that same night they began a cross-country search that would go on for the next five days. But there was no trace of him. The police thought he might have got in to a car with a stranger. He might have been abducted. But nobody had seen anything. It was as if the countryside had taken him and swallowed him up, one policeman said.

Gary watched as the police finally left. He watched as his mother carried her suitcase out of Pye Hall and got into the taxi that would take her back to Ipswich station and her train to London. He was glad to see that she had the decency to cry, mourning her loss. But he couldn't help feeling that she looked rather less tired and rather less ill than she had when she arrived.

Gary's mother did not see him. As she turned round in the taxi to wave goodbye to her mother and Pye Hall, she did notice that this time there were no crows. But then she saw why. They had been scared away by a figure that was standing in the middle of a field, leaning on a stick. For a moment she thought she recognised its torn black and white jacket and the grimy Bart Simpson T-shirt. But she was probably confused. It was best not to say anything.

The taxi accelerated past the new scarecrow and continued down past the poplar trees to the main road.

a career in
COMPUTER
games

A CAREER IN COMPUTER GAMES

Fit, enthusiastic person wanted for development of new computer game. No experience or qualifications needed. Highest salary paid plus bonus. Telephone: 020 8340 1225

It was just a card like all the others, in the window of his local newsagent, but right from the start Kevin knew the job had to be for him. He was sixteen years old and just out of school and there were two things about him that were absolutely true. He had no experience and no qualifications.

Kevin loved games. His pocket computer had gone to school with him every day of the last year, even though it was against school rules, and when it was finally confiscated by a weary teacher in the middle of a geography lesson (just as he'd been about to find the last gold star in Moon Quest) he'd gone straight out and bought another one – this time with a colour screen and had spent the rest of the term playing with that.

Every day when he got home he threw his bag into

the corner, ignoring his homework, and either booted up his dad's lap-top for a game of Brain Dead or Blade of Evil or plugged in his own for a quick session of Road Kill 2. Kevin's bedroom was piled high with computing magazines and posters. It would also be true to say that he had never actually met most of his best friends. He simply exchanged messages with them on the Internet – mainly hints for games, the secret codes and short cuts.

And that wasn't the end of it. On Saturdays, Kevin would take the bus into London and lose himself in the arcades. There was one, right in the heart of Piccadilly, that was three floors high and absolutely crammed with all the latest equipment. Kevin would go up the escalator with his pockets bulging with one-pound coins. To him, there was no sound in the world sweeter than a brand new coin rolling into a slot. By the end of the day, he would stagger home with empty pockets, an empty head and a dazed smile on his face.

The result of all this was that Kevin had finally left school with no knowledge of anything at all. He had failed all his exams – the ones that he'd even bothered to show up for, that is. University was obviously out of the question – he couldn't even have spelled it. And, as he was already discovering, job opportunities for people as ignorant as him were few and far between.

But he wasn't particularly worried. Since the age of thirteen, he'd never been short of money and he saw no reason why this shouldn't continue. Kevin was the youngest of four children living in a large house in Camden Town, north London. His father, a quiet, sad-looking man, did the night shift in a bakery and slept for most of the day so the two of them never met. His mother worked in a shop. He had a brother in the army. A married sister and another brother training to be a taxi-driver. He himself was a thief. And he was good at it.

For that was how he'd got the money to buy himself all the computer equipment and games. That was how he paid for the arcades in town. He'd started with shop-lifting – the local supermarket, the corner shops, the book shop and the chemist in the

High Street. Then he'd met some other kids who'd taught him the riskier – but more profitable – arts of car theft and burglary. There was a pub he knew in Camden Town where he could get five pounds for a car radio, twenty for a decent stereo or video camera, and no questions asked. Kevin had never been caught. And the way he saw it, provided he was careful, he never would be.

Kevin had been passing the newsagent on his way to the pub when he saw the notice. Jobs – that is, honest jobs – didn't interest him. But there was something about the advertisement that did. The 'highest salary and bonus' bit for a start. But it wasn't just that. He knew he was fit. He'd sprinted away from enough smashed car windows and broken back doors to know that. He was certainly enthusiastic, at least when it came to computer games. Of course, he might be wasting his time – if they wanted someone to do programming or anything like that. But...

Why not. Why the hell not?

And that was how, three days later, he found

himself outside an office in Rupert Street, in the middle of Soho. He had come to meet a Miss Toe. That was what she had called herself. Kevin had called her from a telephone box and he'd been so pleased to get an interview that for once he hadn't vandalised the phone. Now, though, he wasn't so sure. The address that she had given him belonged to a narrow, red-bricked building squeezed in between a cake shop and a tobacconist. It was so narrow, in fact, that he'd walked past it twice before he found where it was. It was also very old, with dusty windows and the sort of front door you'd expect to find on a dungeon. There was a small brass plaque beside this. Kevin had to lean down to read it.

GALACTIC GAMES LTD

It wasn't a good start. In all the magazines he'd read, Kevin had never heard of anyone called Galactic Games. And now that he thought of it, what sort of computer games company would be advertising in the window of a newsagent in Camden

Town? What sort of computer company would have a crummy office like this?

He almost decided to go. He'd actually turned round and walked away before he changed his mind. Now that he was here, he might as well go in. After all, he'd paid for a ticket on the Underground (even if he had cheated and bought a child's fare). He had nothing else to do. It would probably be a laugh and if nobody was looking he might be able to nick an ashtray.

He rang the bell.

'Yes?' The voice at the other end of the intercom was high-pitched, a bit sing-song.

'My name's Kevin Graham,' he said. 'I've come about the job.'

'Oh yes. Please come straight up. The first floor.'

The door buzzed and he pushed it open and went in. A narrow flight of stairs in a dark, empty corridor led up. Kevin was liking this less and less. The stairs were crooked. The whole place felt about a hundred years old. And all sound from the street had disappeared from the moment the heavy door had swung shut behind him. Once again he thought about turning around but it was too late. A door opened at the top of the stairs, spilling a golden light into the gloom. A figure appeared, looking down at him.

'Please. This way...'

Kevin reached the door and saw that it had been opened by a small, Japanese-looking woman wearing a plain black dress with black high-heeled shoes that tilted her forward as if she were about to fall flat on her face. Her face, what he could see of it, was round and pale. Black sunglasses covered her eyes. And she really was small. Her head barely came up to his chin.

'So who are you?' he asked.

'I am Miss Toe,' she said. She had a strange accent. It wasn't Japanese but it certainly wasn't English. And as she spoke she left the tiniest of gaps between each word. 'I – am – Miss – Toe. We – spoke – on – the – telephone.' She closed the door.

Kevin found himself in a small office with a single desk bare but for a single phone and with a single chair behind it. There was nothing else in the room.

The walls, recently painted white, didn't have one picture on them, not even a calendar. So much for stealing, he thought to himself. There wasn't anything to take.

'Mr Go will see you now,' she said.

Miss Toe and Mr Go in Soho. Kevin wanted to laugh but for some reason he couldn't. It was too weird.

Mr Go was sitting in an office next to Miss Toe's. It was like walking through a mirror. His room was exactly the same as hers, with bright white walls; one desk, one telephone, but two chairs. Mr Go was the same size as his assistant and also wore dark glasses. He was dressed in a jersey that was slightly too small for him and a pair of cords that was slightly too big. As he stood up, his movements were jerky and he too left gaps between his words.

'Please, come in,' Mr Go said, seeing Kevin at the door. He smiled, revealing a row of teeth with more silver than white. 'Sit down!' He gestured at the chair and Kevin took it, feeling more suspicious by the minute. There was definitely something odd here. Something not quite right. Mr Go reached into his desk and took out a square of paper: some sort of form. Kevin's reading wasn't up to much and anyway the paper was upside down but as far as he could tell the form wasn't written in English. The words were made up of pictures rather than letters and seemed to go down rather than across the page. It had to be Japanese, he supposed.

'What is your name?' Mr Go asked him.

'Kevin Graham.'

'Age?'

'Sixteen.'

'Address?'

Kevin gave it.

'You've left school?'

'Yeah. A couple of months ago.'

'And tell me please. Did you get good GCSEs?'

'No.' Kevin was angry now. 'Your ad said no qualifications needed. That's what it said. So why are you wasting my time asking me?'

Mr Go looked up sharply. It was impossible to tell with the dark glasses covering his eyes, but he seemed to be pleased. 'You're quite right,' he said.

'Quite right. Yes. Qualifications are not required. Not at all. But can you supply references?'

'What do you mean?' Kevin was lounging in his chair. He had decided he didn't care if he got the job or not – and he didn't want this ridiculous Jap to think he did.

'References from your teachers. Or your parents. Or former employers. To tell me what sort of person you are.'

'I've never had an employer,' Kevin said. 'My teachers would just give you a load of rubbish. And my parents can't be bothered. Shove the references! Who needs them anyway?'

Even as he spoke the words, he knew that the interview was probably over. But there was something about the empty room and the small, doll-like man that unnerved him. He wanted to go. To his surprise, Mr Go smiled again and nodded his head vigorously. 'Absolutely!' he agreed. 'The references can indeed be shoved. Although you have only been in my office for a matter of some twenty-nine-and-a-half seconds, I can already see your character for myself. And my dear Kevin – I may call you Kevin? – I can see that it is exactly the sort of character we require. Exactly!'

'What is this place?' Kevin demanded.

'Galactic Games,' Mr Go replied. 'The finest games inventors in the universe. Certainly the most advanced this side of the Milky Way. We've won many, many awards for *Smash Crash Slash 500*. And our new, advanced version (we call it *Smash Crash Slash 500 Plus*) is going to be even better.'

'*Smash Crash Slash?*' Kevin wrinkled his nose. 'I've never heard of it.'

'It hasn't been marketed yet. Not in this…area. But we want you to work on this game. In this game. And if you're game, the job's yours.'

'How much do you pay?' Kevin demanded.

'Two thousand a week plus car plus healthcare plus funeral package.'

'Funeral package?'

'It's just an extra we throw in – not of course that you'll need it.' Mr Go took out a golden pen and scribbled a few notes on the piece of paper, then span it round so that it faced Kevin. 'Sign here,' he said.

Kevin took the pen. It was curiously heavy. But for a moment he hesitated. 'Two thousand a week,' he repeated.

'Yes.'

'What sort of car?'

'Any car you want.'

'But you haven't told me what I have to do. You haven't told me anything about the job…'

Mr Go sighed. 'All right,' he said. 'Right. Right. Right. Never mind. We'll find someone else.'

'Wait a minute…'

'If you're not interested!'

'I am interested.' Kevin had caught the smell of money. Two thousand pounds a week and a car! What did it matter if Mr Go seemed to be completely mad and if he'd never heard of either the company or the game…what was it called? *Bash Smash Dash*. He quickly searched for a clear space on the sheet of paper and scribbled his name.

Kevin Graham…

But the strange thing was that as the pen travelled

across the page, it seemed to become red hot in his hand. It only lasted for a second or two, as long as it took him to form his signature, but no sooner was it done than he cried out and dropped the pen, curling his fingers and holding them up as if to find burn marks. But there was nothing. Mr Go picked up the pen. It was quite cool again. He popped it back into his pocket and slid the sheet of paper back to his side of the desk.

'Well, that's it,' he said. 'Welcome to *Smash Crash Slash 500 Plus*.'

'When do I start?' Kevin asked.

'You already have.' Mr Go stood up. 'We'll be in touch with you very soon,' he said. He gestured. 'Please. Show yourself out.'

Kevin was going to argue. Part of him even thought of punching the little man on the nose. That would show him! But his hand was still smarting from the pen and he very much wanted to get out, back on to the street. Maybe he'd walk over to the Piccadilly arcade. Or maybe he'd just go home and go to bed. Whatever he did, he didn't want to stay here.

He left the room the way he had come.

Miss Toe was no longer in her office but the door was open on the other side and he walked out. And that was when he noticed something else strange. The door was glowing. It was as if there was a neon strip built into the frame. As he walked through it, the light danced in his eyes, dazzling him.

'What on earth...?' he muttered to himself.

He didn't stop walking until he got home.

There weren't many people around as Kevin turned into the street where he lived. It was half past three and most of the mothers would be fetching their kids from school or in the kitchens preparing tea. The ones who weren't at work themselves, of course. Cranwell Grove was actually a crescent; a long, quiet road with Victorian terraced houses standing side by side all the way round. About half the buildings belonged to a Housing Association and Kevin's father had been lucky enough to get the one at the very end of the row, three floors high, stained glass in the front door and ivy growing up the side. Kevin didn't like it there, of course. He argued with the neighbours. (Why did they have to get so uptight about their cat? He'd only thrown the one brick at it...) And it was too quiet for his liking. Too boring and middle class. He'd rather have had his own flat.

He had just reached the front door when he saw the man walking towards him. He wouldn't normally have taken any notice of anyone walking down Cranwell Grove but there were two things about this man that struck him as odd. The first was that he was wearing a suit. The second thing was the speed at which he was walking; a fast, deliberate pace. He was heading for Kevin's house. There could be no doubt of it.

Kevin's first thought was that this was a plain-clothes policeman. With his hand resting on the key which was already in the lock, his mind raced back over the past few weeks. He'd nicked a car stereo from a BMW parked in Camden Road. And then there'd been that bottle of gin that he had slipped out of the off-licence near the station. But neither time had anyone seen him. Could his face have been caught by a video camera? Even if it had been, how had they managed to find him?

The man was closer now, close enough for Kevin to see his face. He shivered. The face was round and expressionless, the mouth a single, horizontal line, the eyes as lifeless as marbles. The man seemed to have had some sort of surgery, plastic surgery that had left him with more plastic than skin. Even his hair could have been painted on.

The man stopped. He was about twenty metres away.

'What do you...?' Kevin began.

The man pulled out a gun.

Kevin stared – more amazed than actually frightened. He had seen guns on television a thousand times. People shot each other all the time in plays and films. But this was different. This man, this total stranger, was just ten paces away. He was standing in Cranwell Grove and he was holding...

The man brought up the weapon and aimed it. Kevin yelled out and ducked. The man fired. The bullet slammed into the door, inches above his head, shattering the wood.

Real bullets!

That was his first, insane thought. This was a real gun with real bullets. His second thought was even more horrible.

The man was aiming again.

Somehow, when Kevin ducked, he'd managed to hold on to the key. It was above his head now, his fingers still clinging around it. Hardly knowing what he was doing, he turned the key in the lock and almost cried with relief as he felt the door open behind him. He leant back and virtually tumbled in as the man fired a second shot, this one snapping into the wall and spitting fragments of sand and brickwork into his face.

He landed with a thud on the hall carpet, twisted round, jerked the key out and slammed the door. For a moment he lay there, panting, his heart beating so hard that he could feel it pushing against his chest. This wasn't happening to him. *What* wasn't happening to him? He tried to collect his thoughts. Some lunatic had escaped from an asylum and had wandered into Cranwell Grove, shooting anything that moved. No. That wasn't right. Kevin remembered how the man had walked towards him. He had been heading straight for Kevin. There was no question about it. It was him the man wanted to kill.

But why? Who was he? Why him?

He heard the sound of feet moving outside. The man hadn't given up! He was getting closer. Desperately, Kevin looked around him. Was he alone in the house?

'Mum!' he called. 'Dad!'

No answer.

He saw the telephone. Of course, he should have thought of it at once. There was a dangerous lunatic outside and he'd wasted precious seconds when he should have been calling the police. He snatched up the receiver but before he had even dialled the first nine, there was a volley of shots that seemed to explode all around him. He stared in horror. From his side, it looked as if the door was tearing itself apart but he knew it was the man out on the pavement, shooting out the lock. Even as he watched, the door handle and lock shuddered and ricocheted on to the carpet. The door swung open.

Kevin did the only thing he could think of. With a shout, he snatched up the table on which the telephone had stood and swung it round in a great arc. And he was lucky. Just as the table reached the door, the man appeared, stepping into the hall. The table smashed right into his face and he fell backwards, crumpling in a heap.

Kevin stood where he was, catching his breath. He was stunned, the gunshots still ringing in his ears, his head reeling. What was he going to do? Oh yes. Ring the police. But the telephone had fallen when he had picked up the table and there it was, smashed on the floor. There was a second phone in his parents' bedroom but that was no use. The door would be locked. His mother had locked it ever since she'd found him stealing from her handbag.

But there *was* a telephone. A box at the end of the street. Better to go there than stay in the house because the man he'd just hit wouldn't stay unconscious for ever. Better not to be around when he woke up. Kevin stepped over the body and went out.

And stopped.

A second man was walking towards him and what was odd, what made it all so nightmarish, was that this man was identical to the first. Not just similar – exactly the same. They could have been two dummies out of the same shop window. Kevin almost giggled at the thought – but it was true. The same dark suit. The same plastic, empty face. The same measured pace. And now the man was reaching into his jacket for...

...the same heavy, silver-plated gun.

'Go away!' Kevin screamed. He lurched backwards into the house just as the man fired off a shot, the bullet drilling through the stained-glass window in the front door and smashing a picture that hung in the hall.

This time Kevin was defenceless. He had already used the telephone table and apart from his mother's umbrella there was nothing else in sight. He had to get away. That was the only thing to do. He was unarmed. Defenceless. He had just been attacked by a lunatic and now it seemed that the lunatic had a twin brother.

Whimpering to himself, Kevin crossed the hall and ran up the stairs, stumbling as he tried to keep his eyes on the front door. He was aware of a sudden shadow and then the man was there, stepping into the opening and firing at the same time. The bullet shot over Kevin's shoulder. Kevin screamed and jumped out of the window.

He hadn't opened it first. Glass and wood exploded all around him, almost blinding him as he fell through the air and landed on all fours on the roof below. There was a lean-to next to the kitchen at the top of the garden and that was where he was now. His wrist was hurting and he saw that he had cut himself. Bright red blood slid over the gap between his thumb and first finger. Grimacing, he pulled a piece of glass out of the side of his arm. He was just glad he hadn't broken an arm or a leg.

Because he was going to need them.

From where Kevin was standing – or crouching, rather – he had a view of all the back gardens, not just of the houses in Cranwell Grove but those of

Addison Road which ran parallel to it. Here everything was green, precise rectangles of lawn separated by crumbling walls and fences and punctuated with greenhouses, sheds, garden furniture and barbecues. He had no time to enjoy the view. Even as he straightened up, he saw them: half-a-dozen more men with guns, all of them identical to the two he had already encountered. They were making their way through the gardens, hoisting themselves over the fences, marching across the lawns.

'Oh no...' he began.

Behind him, the man who had broken through his front door appeared at the shattered window and took aim. Kevin somersaulted forward and landed on his own back lawn, a fall that knocked his breath away and left him dizzy and confused. The man at the window fired. The bullet whacked into a sunflower, chopping it in half. Kevin got to his feet and ran to the far end of the garden, hurled himself over the fence and tumbled, with a furious yell, into his neighbour's goldfish pond.

He was soaking wet. His shoulder was bruised, his

wrist stung from the broken glass, and he was feeling sick and disorientated but sheer terror drove him on. It suddenly occurred to him that from the moment the nightmare had begun, nobody had said a word. There were at least eight men in suits pursuing him but none of them had spoken. And despite the sounds of gunfire on a quiet summer afternoon, none of the residents of Cranwell Grove had come to see what was happening. He had never felt more utterly alone.

Dripping water, Kevin crossed his neighbour's garden and then vaulted over the wall into the next garden along. This one had a gate and he pushed through it, emerging into a narrow alleyway that led back to the road. Limping now – he must have twisted his ankle in the fall from the window – he ran to the end, just in time to hop on to a bus that was pulling out of a stop. Gratefully, he sank into his seat. As the bus picked up speed he looked back out of the window. Four of the men in suits – or maybe it was four new ones – had appeared in Cranwell Grove, and stood in a crowd in the middle of the road. Four shop dummies from C&A, Kevin thought. Despite everything, he felt a surge of pleasure. Whoever they were, he had beaten them. He had left them behind.

And that was when he heard the motor cycles.

They roared out of nowhere, overtaking the four men in suits and pounding up the road towards the bus. There were about nine of them; huge machines, all glinting metalwork and fat, black tyres. The nine riders were dressed in uniform mauve leather, covering them from head to toe. Their heads were covered by silver helmets with black glass completely hiding their faces.

'Oh God...' Kevin whispered.

Nobody on the bus seemed to have noticed him. Despite the fact that he was dirty, his clothes soaked, his hair in disarray and his face covered in sweat, the other passengers were completely ignoring him. Even the bus conductor walked straight past him with a vacant smile.

What was happening to him?

What was going on?

The first of the motor bikes drew level with the bus. The rider reached behind him and pulled a weapon out of a huge holster slung across his shoulders. Kevin gazed through the window, his mouth dropping. The rider had produced some sort of bazooka, a weapon at least three metres long and as thick as a tree-trunk. Kevin whimpered. He reached up to pull the 'Stop' cord. The motor cyclist fired.

There was an explosion so loud that several windows shattered. An elderly woman with a newspaper was propelled out of her seat. Kevin saw her hurtle through the air from the very front of the bus to the back where she landed and cheerfully went on reading. The bus careered to the left, mounted the pavement and crashed into the window of a supermarket. Kevin covered his eyes and screamed. He felt the world spinning round him as the wheels of the bus screeched and slid across the supermarket floor. Something soft hit him on the shoulder and he opened one eye to glimpse an avalanche of toilet paper cascading down on him through the hole that the biker had blasted in the bus. The bus was still moving, drilling through the interior of the supermarket. It smashed through breakfast cereals, dairy products and bakery, skidded into soft drinks and frozen vegetables and finally came to a halt in dog food.

Kevin opened his other eye, grateful that it was still there. He was covered in broken glass, fallen plaster, dust and toilet paper. The other passengers were still sitting in their seats, gazing out of the windows and looking only mildly surprised that the driver had decided to take a short cut through a supermarket.

'What's the matter with you?' Kevin screamed. 'Can't you see what's going on?'

Nobody said anything. But the old lady who had been rocketed out of her seat turned a page and smiled at him vaguely.

Outside the supermarket, the motor cycles waited, parked in a perfect semicircle. The drivers dismounted and began to walk towards what was left of the window. Kevin let out a sob and got shakily to his feet. He just had time to throw himself out of the wreckage of the bus before the whole vehicle disappeared in a barrage of explosions, the bazookas ripping it apart as if it were nothing more than a large red paper box.

How he got out of the supermarket he would never know. In all the dust and the confusion he could barely see and the noise of the bazookas had utterly deafened him. All he knew was that somehow he had to survive. He leapt over the cheese counter – but not quite far enough. One foot plopped down in a loose Camembert and he was nearly thrown flat on his back. There was a door on the other side and he reeled through it, dragging a foot which not only hurt but which now smelled of ripe French cheese. There was a storeroom on the other side and a loading bay beyond that. Two men in white coats were unloading a delivery of fresh meat. They ignored him.

Fresh meat. Suddenly Kevin knew how it felt.

Somehow he made it to Camden High Street, dodging up alleyways and crouching behind parked cars, desperately looking out for men in black suits and men on motor bikes. Three yellow helicopters were buzzing overhead now and somehow, just looking at them, he knew they were part of it too.

Perhaps it was intuition. Or perhaps it was the fact that they had 'Kill Kevin Graham' written in red letters on their sides. But he knew they were the enemy. They were looking for him.

He had two more narrow escapes.

One of the bikers spotted him outside Waterstone's and fired off a rocket that just missed him, completely destroying the book shop and littering the High Street with a blizzard of burning pages. He was almost killed a few seconds later by one of the helicopters firing an air-to-ground heat-seeking missile. It should have locked on to Kevin's body heat and disintegrated him in a single, vast explosion, but he was lucky. He had been standing next to an electricity showroom and the missile was confused at the last moment by the electric fires on display. It snaked over his shoulder and into the shop, utterly destroying it and three other buildings in the same arcade and although Kevin was blown several metres away by the force of the blast, he wasn't seriously hurt.

By the time the clock struck nine, there was nothing left in the High Street that you could actually call high.

Most of the shops had been reduced to piles of rubble. The bus stops and street-lamps had been snapped in half, pillar-boxes uprooted and prefabricated offices de-fabricated and demolished. And when the clock did strike nine it was itself struck by a thermonuclear warhead, fired by one of the helicopters, and blown to smithereens. At least the mauve-suited bikers were nowhere to be seen. It would have been impossible to drive up Camden High Street in anything but a tractor. There wasn't much street left – just a series of huge holes. On the other hand, their place had now been taken by a swarm of green and silver flying dragons with scorpion tails, razor-sharp claws and searchlight eyes. The dragons were incinerating anything that moved. But nothing was moving. Night had fallen and Camden Town with it.

Kevin Graham was squatting in one of the bomb craters. His clothes were rags – his jeans missing one entire leg – and his body was streaked with blood, fresh and dry. There was a cut over his eye and a bald patch at the back of his head where a large part of his hair had been burned off. His eyes were red. He had been crying. His tears left dirty tracks down his cheeks. He was lying underneath a mattress that had been blown out of a bed shop. He was grateful for it. It hid him from the helicopters and from the dragons. It was the only soft thing left in his world.

He must have fallen asleep because the next thing he knew, it was light. The morning sun had risen and everything around him was silent. With a shiver, he heaved the mattress off him and stood up. He listened for a moment, then climbed out of the crater.

It was true. The nightmare was over. The armies that had spent the whole day trying to kill him had disappeared. He stretched his legs, feeling the warm sun on his back, and gazed around him at the smouldering mess that had once been a prosperous north London suburb. Well, that didn't matter. To hell with Camden Town. He was alive!

And he had finally worked out what he had to do.

He had to make his way back into town and find the offices of Galactic Games. He had to tell Mr Go that it had all been a mistake, that he didn't want a career in computer games, that he wasn't interested in *Smash Crash Slash 500*, even if it was the most popular game in the universe. And he believed that now. He just wondered from which part of the universe Mr Go had come.

That was what he would do. Mr Go would understand. He'd tear up the contract and it would all be over.

Kevin took a step forward and stopped.

Overhead, he heard a sound like thunder. For a moment it filled the air – a strange rolling, booming, followed by a pause and then a metallic crash.

A summer storm?

At the far end of the battlefield, a man in a black suit appeared and began to walk towards him.

Kevin felt his legs turn to jelly. His eyes watered and a sob cracked in his throat. He knew that sound all right. He knew it all too well.

The sound of an arcade.

And someone, somewhere, had just put in another coin.

howard's
END

Howard Blake didn't even see the bus that ran him over.

Nor did he feel it. One minute he was running across Oxford Street with a stack of CDs in his hand and the clang of the alarm bell ringing in his ears and the next…nothing. That was the trouble with shoplifting of course. When you were caught you just had to run and you couldn't stop at the edge of the road for such niceties as looking left and right. You just had to go for it. Howard had gone for it but unfortunately he hadn't made it. The bus had hit him halfway across the road. And here he was. Fifteen years old and already dead.

He opened his eyes.

'Blimey!' he croaked. 'This isn't happening.'

He closed them again, counted to ten, then slowly opened them, one at a time. There could be no doubt about it. Unless this was some sort of hallucination, he was no longer in London. He was…

'Oh blimey!' he whispered again.

He was still wearing the same black leather jacket, T-shirt and jeans but he was sitting on a billowing white substance that looked suspiciously like a cloud. No. He couldn't pretend. It was a cloud. The air was warm and smelled of flowers and he could hear music, soft notes being plucked out on the strings of what he knew must be harps. About thirty metres away from him there was a pair of gates, solid gold, encrusted with dazzling white pearls. Light was pouring through the bars, making it hard to see what was on the other side. And there was something strange about the light. Although it looked very much like sunshine, the sky was actually dark. When Howard looked up he could see thousands of stars, set against a backdrop of the deepest, darkest blue. It seemed to be both night and day at the same time.

Howard was not alone. There was a queue stretching back as far as he could see...stretching so far that even the people in the middle were no bigger than pinpricks. Looking at the ones who were closer to him, he saw that there were men and women from just about every country in the world and dressed in an extraordinary variety of clothes from three-piece suits to saris, kimonos and even eskimo furs. A great many of them were old but there were also teenagers and even young children among them. They were waiting quietly, as if they had always expected to end up here and were cheerfully resigned now that they'd arrived.

But arrived where?

The answer, of course, was obvious. Howard had only ever been to church once and that was to steal the silver candlesticks on the altar, but even he got the general idea. The queue, the clouds, the harps, the pearly gates…it took him right back to Cross Street Comprehensive and Religious Education classes with Doris Witherspoon. So the old bat had been right after all! There was such a thing as heaven. The thought almost made him giggle. 'Our Father who art in heaven…' How did the rest of the prayer go? He'd forgotten. But the point was, he'd always assumed that heaven and hell were just places they made up to scare you into being good. It was remarkable to discover that it was actually true.

He stood up, his feet sinking gently into the cloud which shifted to take his weight. Howard was not particularly bright. He'd only been to school half a dozen times that year and had fully intended to stop altogether as soon as he turned sixteen, but now his brain began to grind into motion. He was in a queue of people outside the gates of heaven. All the people were presumably dead. So it had to follow that he must be dead too. But how had it happened? He couldn't remember being murdered or anything like that. Had he been ill? It was true he'd smoked at least ten cigarettes a day for as long as he could remember, and his mother was always warning him he'd get cancer – but surely he'd have noticed if it had actually happened.

He thought back. That morning he'd woken up in his house on the estate where he lived just outside Watford. He'd eaten his breakfast, kicked the dog, sworn at his mother and gone to school. Of course he hadn't actually arrived at the school. He'd missed so many days that the social workers had been round looking for him but as usual he'd given them the slip. He'd gone into town. That's right. Cheated on the tube train, buying a child's fare, then gone to the West End. He'd eaten a second breakfast in a greasy spoon, then gone to a little snooker club behind Goodge Street...the sort of place that didn't ask too many questions when he went in, and certainly not about his age. He'd thought of going to the new James Bond film but he had an hour to kill before it started so he'd decided to do a little shoplifting instead. There were plenty of big stores on Oxford Street. The bigger the store, the easier the snatch. He'd slipped a couple of CDs under his jacket and was just picking out some more when he'd noticed the store detective closing in on him. So he'd run. And...

What had happened? Now that he thought about it, he had seen a blur of red out of the corner of his eye. There'd been a rush of wind and something had nudged his shoulder, very gently. And that was it. That was the last thing he remembered.

However he looked at it, there could only be one answer. He had been killed! No doubt about it! And...

The next thoughts came very quickly, all in a jumble.

Heaven exists. So hell exists. You don't want to go to hell. You want to go to heaven. But there's no way you're going to heaven, mate. Not with your record. Not unless you manage something pretty spectacular. You're going to have to pull the wool over their eyes good and proper and the sooner you get started...

Howard pushed his way into the queue, stepping between a small Chinese man with the ivory hilt of a knife protruding from his chest, and an old woman who was still wearing her hospital identity bracelet.

'What are you doing?' the woman demanded.

'Get lost, grandma,' Howard replied. Even though all the cigarettes had stunted his growth, Howard was still thick-set and muscular. He had a pale face, greasy hair and dark, ugly eyes which – along with his black leather jacket and the silver studs in his ears, left cheek, nose and lip – made him look dangerous. He wasn't the sort of person you argued with, even if you could see that he was no longer alive. True to form the old lady fell silent.

The queue shuffled forward. Now Howard could

make out a figure sitting on a sort of high stool beside the gates. It was an ancient man with long white hair and a tumbling beard. Dress him in red, Howard thought, and you'd have a heavenly version of Father Christmas. But in fact his robes were white. He was holding a large book, a sort of ledger, and there was a bunch of keys tied around his waist. The man turned briefly and Howard was astonished to see two huge wings sprouting out of his back, the brilliant white feathers tapering down behind him. There were two younger men with him and Howard realised with a shiver that he knew who – or at least what – they were. The keepers of the keys. The guardians at the gates of heaven. He threw his mind back, trying desperately to remember what Miss Witherspoon had said. What was the man with the keys called? Bob? Patrick? Percy? No – it was Peter! Saint Peter! That was it! That was the guy he had to persuade to let him in.

It took another hour but at last he reached the gates. By now, Howard had composed himself. He could see heaven in front of him. But he could imagine hell. He knew which he preferred.

'Name?' St Peter (it had to be him) asked.

'Howard,' Howard replied. 'Howard Blake, sir.' He was pleased with the 'sir'. He had to show respect. Butter the old fool up.

'How old are you, Howard?'

'I'm fifteen, sir.' Howard tried to sound very young and innocent. He wished now that he had thought to remove all the silver pins from his face.

One of the younger angels leant forward and whispered to Saint Peter. The old angel nodded. 'You were killed on Oxford Street, this afternoon,' he said.

'Yes, sir. I can't imagine what my old mum will say. It'll break her heart, I'm sure...'

'Why weren't you in school?'

Howard swallowed. If he told them he was playing truant, he'd be done for. He had to think of something. 'Well, sir...' he gurgled. 'It was my mum's birthday. So I asked the teacher if I could take the afternoon to nick something for her...I mean, buy something for her. I wanted to buy her something nice. So I popped into town.'

'Were you always kind to your mother, child?'

Howard remembered all the names he had called her that morning. He thought of the money he had stolen from her handbag. Sometimes he'd stolen the entire handbag too. 'I tried to be a good boy,' he said.

'And did you work hard at school?'

'Oh yes. School is very important. Religious education was always my favourite lesson. And I worked as hard as I could, sir.'

'You look like a strong boy. I hope you never bullied anyone.'

Images flashed in front of Howard's eyes. Glen Roven with a black eye. Robin Addison, crying, with a bleeding nose. Blake Ewing with a twisted arm, shouting while Howard stole his lunch money. 'Oh never, sir,' he replied. 'I hate bullies.'

'Hatred is a sin, child.'

'Is it? Well, I quite like bullies, really. I just don't like what they do!'

Howard was sweating, but the angel seemed content. He made a few notes in his book. He was using a feather pen, Howard noticed. He wondered if the angel had made it out of his own wing.

St Peter peered at him closely and for a moment Howard was forced to look away. The angel's eyes seemed to look right into him and even through him. He wondered how many thousands – how many millions of people those eyes had examined.

'Do you repent your sins?' St Peter asked.

'Sins? I never sinned!' Howard felt his hand curling into a fist and quickly unclenched it. He somehow didn't think it would be a good idea to punch St Peter on the nose. 'Well, maybe I forgot to feed the dog once or twice,' he said. 'And I didn't do my maths homework one evening last June. I repent about that. But that's it, sir. There ain't nothing more.'

There was a soft clunk and Howard noticed that one of the CDs he had been stealing had fallen out of his leather jacket. He glanced at it, blushing. 'Cor! Look at that!' he said. 'I wonder how that got there?' He picked it up and handed it to St Peter. 'Would you like it, sir? It's Heavy Vomit. They're my favourite group.'

St Peter took the CD, glanced at it briefly, then handed it to one of his aides. He smiled. 'All right, my child,' he said. 'You may go through the gates.'

'I may?' Howard was amazed.

'Enter!'

'Thanks a bunch, sir. God bless you and all the rest of it!'

He had done it! He could hardly believe it. He had smiled and simpered and called St Peter 'sir' and the old geezer had actually bought it. And his reward was going to be heaven! Howard straightened his shoulders. Ahead of him, the gates opened. There was swirl of music as a thousand harps came together in a billowing, flowing crescendo. The music seemed to scoop him up in its arms and carry him forward. At the same time he heard singing, like a heavenly choir. No! It *was* a heavenly choir, ten thousand voices, invisible and eternal, singing out in celestial stereo. The light danced in his eyes, washing through him. He walked on, noticing that his black leather jacket and jeans had fallen away to be replaced by his very own white robe and sandals. He passed through the gates and saw them swing gently shut behind him. There was a click and then it was over. The gates had closed. He was in!

The next few days passed very happily for Howard.

He floated along through a landscape of perfect white clouds where the sun never set, where it never rained and where it was never too hot or too cold. Harp music and the soft chanting of hallelujahs filled the great silence. There wasn't any food or water but that didn't matter because he was never hungry or thirsty. It occurred to him that although there must have been millions and millions of people in heaven, the place was so vast that he didn't see many of them. He did pass a few people who waved at him and smiled pleasantly but he ignored them. He was glad to be there with the other angels but that didn't mean he actually had to talk to them.

It was heaven. Sheer heaven.

The days became weeks and the weeks months. The harps continued to play soft, tinkling music that followed Howard everywhere. The truth was, he was getting a little bit fed up with the harps. Didn't they have drums or electric guitars in heaven? He was also a little sorry that heaven didn't have more colour.

White clouds and blue sky were all very well but after a while it was just a bit...repetitive.

He set out now to meet other people deciding that, after all, he would probably enjoy the place more if he wasn't on his own. Certainly the angels were very friendly. Everybody smiled at him. They always seemed happy to see him. But at the same time they didn't have a whole lot to say beyond 'Good morning!' and 'How are you?' and (at least a hundred times a day) 'God bless you!'

Despite the fact that everything was unquestionably perfect, Howard was getting bored and after he had been there for...well, it could have been a year or it could have been ten – it was hard to tell when nothing at all was really happening – he decided that he would purposefully pick a fight, just to see what happened.

He waited until he had found an angel smaller than himself (old habits die hard) and stumped over to him.

'You're very ugly!' he exclaimed.

'I'm sorry?' The angel had been sitting on a cloud

doing nothing in particular. But then, of course, there was nothing particular to do.

'Your face makes me sick,' Howard said.

'I do apologise,' the angel replied. 'I'll leave at once.'

'Are you chicken?' Howard cried.

'Am I a chicken?'

'You're scared!'

'Yes. You're absolutely right.'

The angel tried to leave and that was when Howard hit him, once, hard. The angel jerked back, surprised. Howard's fist had caught him square on the chin but there was no blood, no bruising. There wasn't even any pain. It took the angel a moment or two to realise what had happened. Then he gazed sadly at Howard. 'I forgive you,' he said.

'I don't want to be forgiven!' Howard exclaimed. 'I want to have a fight.'

'God bless you!' the angel said, and drifted away.

Another thousand years passed.

The harps were still playing. The clouds were still a

perfect, whiter-than-white white. The sky was still blue. The weather hadn't changed, not even a little drizzle for just a minute or two. The choirs sang and the angels wandered along, smiling dreamily and blessing one another.

Howard was tearing his hair out. He had torn it out several times, in fact, but it always grew again. He kicked at a cloud and bit his lip as his foot passed right through it. He hadn't been ill, not once in all the time he had been here. He would have quite liked it really. A cough or a cold. Even a bout of malaria. Anything for a change. Nor had he found anyone to talk to. The other angels were all so...boring! Recently – about a hundred and twenty years ago – he had started talking to himself but he had already discovered that he also bored himself – and anyway he hated the sound of his own voice. He had been in a few more fights but they had all ended as disappointingly as the first and he had finally decided there was no point.

And then, quite by chance one day (he had no idea which day and as there was no night he wasn't even sure if it was a day) he realised that he had somehow made his way back to where it had all begun. There were the pearly gates, and standing with his two helpers, there was St Peter, still dealing with the queue that stretched to the horizon and beyond. With the first spurt of hope and excitement he had felt in centuries, Howard hurried forward, the sandals flapping on his feet, his white robes billowing around him.

'Excuse me!' he cried, interrupting St Peter as he talked to a man with a kilt but no legs. 'Excuse me, sir!'

'Yes?' St Peter turned to him and smiled through the bars of the gate.

'You probably don't remember me. But my name is Howard... Howard um...' Howard realised that he had forgotten his own surname. 'I came here quite a long time ago.'

'I remember perfectly well,' St Peter said.

'Well. I have to tell you something!' Suddenly Howard was angry. He'd had enough. More than enough. 'Everything I said when I came here was a lie. I didn't go to school and when I did go to school I bullied everyone, including the teachers. I kicked the cat – or maybe it was a dog. I hated my mum and she hated me. I lied and I cheated and I stole and I know I said I was sorry for what I'd done but I was lying then too because I'm not. I'm glad I did it. I enjoyed doing it.'

'What are you trying to say?' St Peter asked.

'What I'm saying, you horrible old man, is that I don't like it here!' Howard was almost shouting now. 'In fact I hate it here and I've decided I don't want to stay!'

'I'm afraid you have no choice,' St Peter replied. 'That decision is no longer yours.'

'But you don't understand, you bearded twit!' Howard took a deep breath. 'I'm all wrong for heaven. I shouldn't be in heaven. You should never have let me in.'

The angel didn't speak. Howard stared at him. His face had changed. The beard had slipped, like something you buy at a novelty store. Underneath, the chin was pointed and seemed to be covered in what looked suspiciously like scales. And now that he looked more closely, Howard noticed that there was something poking through the old man's hair. Horns?

'Wait...' he began.

St Peter – or whoever, whatever he really was – began to laugh. Two red flames flickered in his eyes and his lips had drawn back to reveal teeth that were viciously sharp.

'My dear Howard,' he said. 'What on earth made you think you'd gone to heaven?'

More Orchard Black Apples

Orchard Black Apples are available from all good bookshops,
or can be ordered direct from the publisher:
Orchard Books, PO BOX 29, Douglas IM99 1BQ
Credit card orders please telephone 01624 836000
or fax 01624 837033 or visit our website:
www.orchardbooks.co.uk
e-mail: bookshop@enterprise.net for details.

rder please quote title, author and ISBN
and your full name and address.
orders should be made payable to 'Bookpost plc.'
and packing is FREE within the UK
tomers should add £2.00 per book).

ilability are subject to change.